Tye May and the Magic Brush

ADAPTED FROM
THE CHINESE BY

Molly Garrett Bang

**A MULBERRY
PAPERBACK BOOK**
New York

TO MY SISTER CAROLINE
AND HER DAUGHTER KLEE

With special thanks to Anna Malmude

Printed in Hong Kong   First Mulberry Edition, 1992

17 19 20 18 16

Library of Congress Cataloging in Publication Data
Bang, Molly. Tye May and the magic brush.
(Greenwillow read-alone books)
Summary: In a dream a poor orphan is given a
brush that brings to life everything she paints.
[1. Painting—Fiction.   2. Magic-Fiction.
3. Orphans—Fiction]   I. Title.
PZ7B2217Ty [E] 80-16488
ISBN 0-688-11504-7

CONTENTS

1 TYE MAY
LEARNS TO DRAW

Many years ago
a cruel and greedy emperor
ruled over China.
His people were very poor.
One of the poorest was Tye May.
Her mother and father were dead,
and she lived alone.
Every day she gathered firewood
and cut reeds
to sell in the marketplace.

One day Tye May

passed by the school.

She saw the teacher painting

and stopped to watch.

She knew, right then,

that was what she wanted to do.

"Please, sir," she said to the teacher,

"I would like to learn how to paint,

but I have no money

to buy a brush.

Would you lend me one?"

The teacher turned red with anger.

"Beggar girls don't paint," he said.

"Get out of here!"

When people saw
her drawings of fish,
they thought the fish
would swim away.

When they saw
her pictures of birds,
they thought the birds
were going to sing.

But still Tye May had no brush.
Every night she thought
how happy she would be
if she could have one.

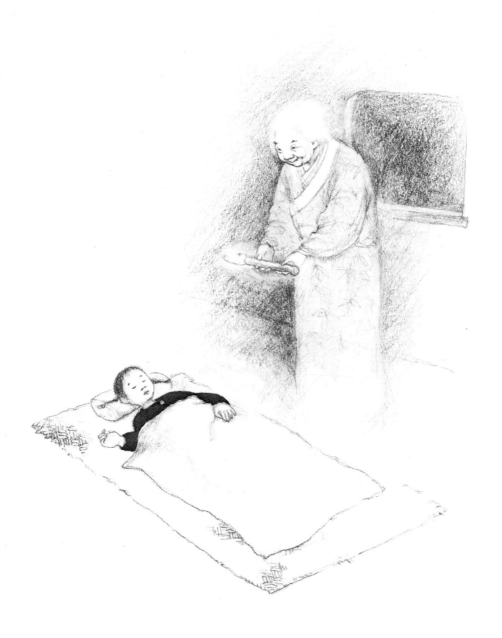

2 THE MAGIC BRUSH

Tye May worked
especially hard one day,
and drew until late at night.
She fell into a deep sleep.
A woman appeared
and held out a brush to her.
"This is a magic brush,"
the woman said.
"Use it carefully."
Tye May took it in her hands.
The brush was soft and thick,
and the handle was
of glittering gold.
It felt heavy and good.

"Thank you, thank you,"

she cried.

But the woman was gone.

Tye May woke up.

It was dawn.

She looked around.

Everything was the same.

She saw the same dirt floor,

the same broken walls,

the same straw mat.

It had all been a dream.

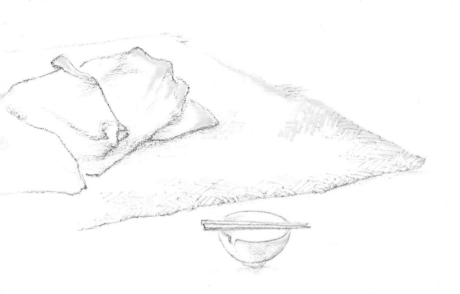

But what was this brush
in her hands?
Tye May was lost in wonder.

She painted a bird.

The bird flew up,

perched outside her window,

and began to sing to her.

It was alive!

She ran outside

and painted a fish.

The fish flipped its tail,

jumped into the river,

and splashed in the water

for her to see.

Tye May was happy.

3 THE WICKED LANDLORD

Soon Tye May began
to use the brush
to make things for the poor.
For a weaver she painted a loom.
For a farmer she painted a hoe,
a pail, and an oxcart.

Before long, a wicked landlord
heard about the magic brush.
He sent for Tye May.
"Paint me a picture," he ordered.
Tye May refused.

The landlord shut her
in an empty stable.
That night it began to snow.
It snowed for three days.
"Now she is cold and hungry,"
thought the wicked landlord.
"Now she will paint for me."
He unlocked the stable door.

Tye May was sitting
in front of a warm stove,
eating hot cakes!
They smelled delicious, too.
The landlord shook with rage.
He ordered six strong men
to kill the girl

and bring him the magic brush.
Tye May heard the men coming.
She painted herself a horse
and galloped away down the road.

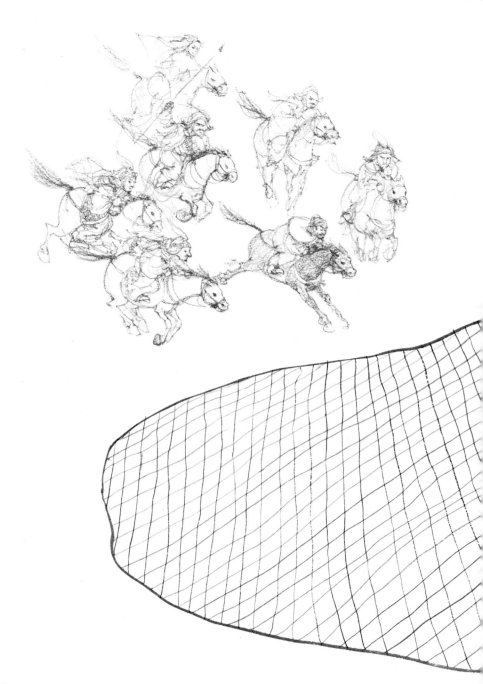

The landlord and his men
mounted their horses
and galloped after her.
They were coming closer and closer.
Tye May stopped her horse.
She jumped down
and painted a big net on the road.

The horses rode into it,
and the men were tangled
in the ropes.
Tye May tied up the net
and rode away.

4 THE EVIL EMPEROR

Tye May rode on for days and nights
until she came to a distant town.
She decided to paint pictures
and sell them in the marketplace.
But she knew it would not be safe
to let people know
about the magic brush.
She painted birds without beaks
and foxes with three legs.
Because the pictures were not whole,
they could not come to life.
No one found out
what the magic brush could do.

One spring day, Tye May
painted a crane,
and left out its eyes, as usual.
But as she passed the brush
over the picture,
two drops of ink
fell onto the bird's head.

They became eyes.

The crane opened them,

lifted its wings,

and flew off over the marketplace.

Everyone stared after the bird.

Now the secret was known.

The Emperor was told,

and he sent his officers

to bring Tye May to court.

Tye May knew

that this Emperor was greedy

and cruel to the poor.

She hated him.

"Paint me a dragon,"

the Emperor commanded.

Tye May painted a toad.

"Paint me a firebird,"

he commanded.

Tye May painted a rooster.

The rooster crowed

and flew onto the Emperor's head.

The toad hopped onto his belly.

They flew and hopped

all over the palace,

and left their droppings everywhere.

The whole palace stank.

The Emperor was furious.

He grabbed the magic brush

and had Tye May

thrown into prison.

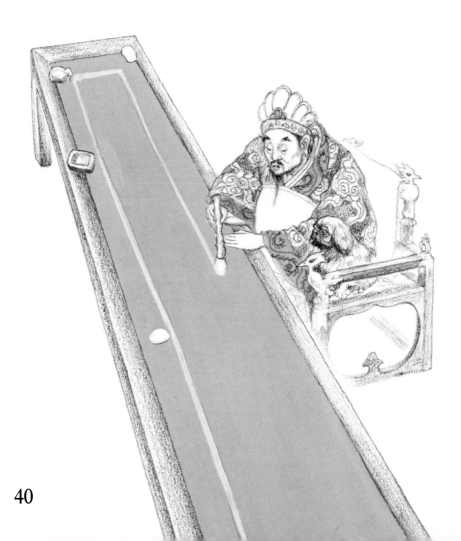

5 THE EMPEROR
TRIES THE BRUSH

The greedy Emperor

tried to use the brush himself.

He painted a big gold brick.

But it was too short.

He painted another.

It was still too short.

Then he painted a long,

long, long, long golden brick,

as long as the whole scroll of paper.

At once the golden brick
became a golden python.
It opened its red mouth
and slid toward the Emperor.

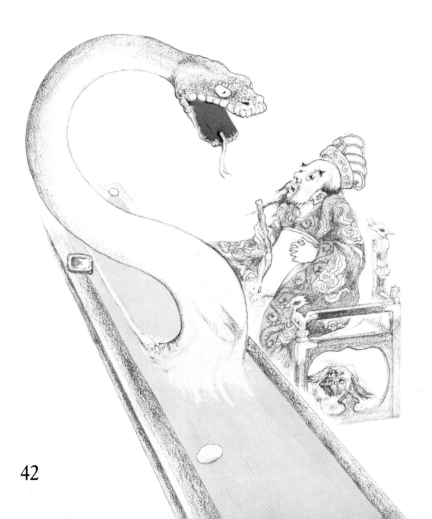

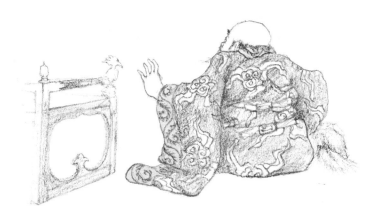

The Emperor fainted,

and the snake disappeared.

The Emperor woke up and trembled.

The Emperor set Tye May free

and begged her to paint for him.

He promised her gold and silver.

He promised her silks and jewels.

He promised her a handsome prince.

Tye May pretended to agree.

"What would you like me
to paint?" she asked.

The Emperor thought about this.

He was still very greedy.

He wanted something big,

but he was also afraid.

If he asked for a mountain,

wild beasts might come out of it

and eat him up.

"Paint me the ocean,"

he commanded.

Tye May painted the ocean.

It was wide and calm,

and smooth as a jade mirror.

The water was so clear the Emperor

could see to the very bottom.

"Why are there no fish?" he asked.

Tye May made a few dots.
The dots became fish
of all the colors of the rainbow.
They wiggled their tails,
splashed back and forth,
and swam slowly out to sea.
The Emperor watched happily.
"Paint me a boat," he commanded.

"I want to sail out

and watch those fish."

Tye May painted a great ship.

The Emperor and Empress,

the Princes and Princesses,

and all their court went on board.

Tye May painted a few strokes.

A breeze blew,

ripples appeared on the water,

and the ship moved off.

6 THE STORM

The ship sailed too slowly
for the Emperor.
He stood on the bow
and called to shore,
"Make the wind blow stronger.
Stronger!"
Tye May painted a few strokes.
A strong wind began to blow
and the seas grew rough.
Tye May painted on.
The wind howled,
the waves rose higher,
and the ship began to roll.

"Enough wind!" the Emperor shouted.
"Enough! Enough!"
Tye May paid no attention.
The winds blew into a terrible storm
and drove the ship across the ocean
to a lonely island.
The ship crashed on the rocks,

and the Emperor and his court
almost drowned.
No ships came to the island
and they were never rescued.
They had to work hard every day,
and were poor
all the rest of their lives.

The story of Tye May

and her magic brush

was told throughout the land.

But what became of her?

No one knows for certain.

Some say that she returned

to the village where she was born.

Others say

she still walks from place to place,

and paints for the poor

wherever she goes.

Chinese characters on title page

| LITTLE | IRON | PLUM FLOWER | RECEIVES | MAGIC | BRUSH |

(Tye May, pronounced Tiéh May, means Iron Plum Flower)

MOLLY BANG grew up in Baltimore, Maryland. She is also the author-illustrator of *Wiley and the Hairy Man* (a 1976 American Library Association Notable Book), *The Grey Lady and the Strawberry Snatcher* (a 1981 Caldecott Honor Book), *Dawn* (a 1984 *Boston Globe–Horn Book* Honor Book), and *Ten, Nine, Eight* (a 1984 Caldecott Honor Book), as well as *The Paper Crane* (winner of the 1986 *Boston Globe–Horn Book* Award for Illustration and a Reading Rainbow Feature Book). Ms. Bang now lives in Woods Hole, Massachusetts.